Croc and Ally

For Aunt Sharon, Uncle Orlin,

Aunt Karmen, and Uncle Gaylord—DA

PENGUIN WORKSHOP
Penguin Young Readers Group
An Imprint of Penguin Random House LLC

Copyright © 2018 by Derek Anderson. All rights reserved.
Published by Penguin Workshop, an imprint of Penguin Random House LLC,
345 Hudson Street, New York, New York 10014. PENGUIN and PENGUIN WORKSHOP are trademarks
of Penguin Books Ltd, and the W colophon is a trademark of Penguin Random House LLC.
Manufactured in China.

Designed by Julia Rosenfeld

Library of Congress Cataloging-in-Publication Data is available.

ISBN 9781524787073   10 9 8 7 6 5 4 3 2 1

Croc and Ally

Friends Forever

by Derek Anderson

Penguin Workshop
An Imprint of Penguin Random House

Move Over

"Will you please move over?

You're hogging the whole sofa,"

said Croc.

"I like to be close to you," said Ally.

"That does it," said Croc.

"Come on, we're going to trade

this sofa for two chairs."

"You can pick out any chair
you want!" said Croc.

Ally sat on all the chairs.

A hard one.

A soft one.

A tall one.

A funny one.

Ally picked the perfect chair.

Croc picked a chair, too.

"Do you like your new chair?"

said Croc.

"I like it," said Ally.

"But I like my chair more

when it is next to your chair."

Mr. Grumpy Pants

Croc was grumpy.

He was grumpy with the rain.

He was grumpy with the mud.

He was grumpy with the bugs.

He was grumpy with Ally.

"Why are you so grumpy?"

said Ally.

"Hrrumph," grumped Croc.

"Do you want to see

what you look like?

I will show you," said Ally.

"Look at me," said Ally.

"I'm grumpy. Hrrumph."

"Do you want to see

what *you* look like?

I will show *you*," said Croc.

"Look at me!

I'm *so* happy.

I love *everything*!"

"You look very happy," said Ally.

"How do you feel?"

"Hrrumph," said Croc.

23

The Moon Is Hiding

"Where is the moon?" asked Ally.

"I don't know," said Croc.

"It must be hiding."

"I can't go to sleep until I find it," said Ally.

"We have to find it!"

"Okay," said Croc.

Croc and Ally looked
in the trees.

Croc and Ally looked in the pond.

Croc and Ally looked

under the rocks.

But they couldn't find it.

The moon had a very good

hiding place.

"I know where to look," said Croc.

"There it is," said Ally.

"Thanks, Croc.

You are a good friend."

"I know," said Croc.

"You are a good friend, too."